Tucker Took It!

Bruce Van Patter

BOYDS MILLS PRESS

HONESDALE, PENNSYLVANIA

To Tom, Andrea and their crew —
who always love a good surprise

—B. V. P.

Text and illustrations copyright © 2010 by Bruce Van Patter

Boyds Mills Press, Inc.
815 Church Street
Honesdale, Pennsylvania 18431
Printed in the United States of America

Library of Congress Cataloging-in-Publication Data

Van Patter, Bruce.
Tucker took it / Bruce Van Patter. — 1st ed.
p. cm.
Summary: When the corn on the farm is ripe,
Tucker the goat comes up with an ingenious way to get some.
ISBN 978-1-59078-698-7 (hardcover : alk. paper)
[1. Goats—Fiction. 2. Food habits—Fiction. 3. Farm life—Fiction.
4. Humorous stories.] I. Title.
PZ7.V346Tu 2010
[E]—dc22
2009020361

First edition
The text of this book is set in 16-point Rockwell.
The illustrations are done digitally.

10 9 8 7 6 5 4 3 2 1

Some people say that goats will eat anything.
That was certainly true about Tucker.

There was, however, one food he liked best: corn,
picked fresh from the stalk. The corn was almost ready.

Oh, how hungry Tucker was. He had waited so long.
It seemed as if he might never get any corn.

What was a hungry goat to do?

One morning, all was quiet on Mrs. Zook's farm.

Sadie the horse knew the sun would soon be hot.

She was glad to have the shade of her straw hat. But . . .

Tucker took it!

Still thinking about his corn, the hungry goat was not satisfied.

Later that morning, three pigs argued about the best time to eat the watermelon Mrs. Zook had given them.

Just when they decided to save it for supper . . .

Tucker took it!

"I'm not finished yet," Tucker thought as the watermelon juice dribbled down his chin.

At noon, Wanda dozed in the cool barn, dreaming about

the sweet hay she would soon munch for lunch. But . . .

Tucker took it!

The goat chewed on some hay and
wanted something else.

With the sun high in the sky, Mrs. Zook hung up her laundry.

Her best sundress fluttered in the breeze and soon would be dry. But . . .

Tucker took it!

"I've got room for one more thing," Tucker thought.

Soon, Mrs. Zook found three unhappy animals by her porch.
"Why, what's wrong, dears?" she asked.
She carefully put her pie down on the table. But . . .

Oh, that Tucker!

"Well, well," said Mrs. Zook. "I can see we're all Tuckered out."

And off she went to get her goat.

She found him by the cornfield.
"Tucker, what have you been up to?" she demanded.

Then Tucker stuck it.

"Next time you need something, Tucker," said Mrs. Zook, "just ask."